I Hear the Train

American Indian Literature and Critical Studies Series
Gerald Vizenor, General Editor

I Hear the Train

Reflections, Inventions, Refractions

Louis Owens

University of Oklahoma Press : Norman

Some of the pieces included here, though revised for this collection, have previously appeared elsewhere: "Soul-Catcher" as "Nalusachito" in *South Dakota Review* (1984); "The Dancing Poodle of Arles" in *Jeopardy* (1985); "Winter Rain" in *Asylum* (1985); "Shelter" in *CUBE Literary Magazine* (1988); "Finding Gene" in *Weber Studies* (fall 1999); "Staging *indians*" as "The Last Man of the Stone Age" in *Loosening the Seams: Interpretations of Gerald Vizenor*, ed. A. Robert Lee (Bowling Green, Ohio: Popular Press, 2000); "Blessed Sunshine" in *Nothing But the Truth: An Anthology of Native American Literature*, ed. John Purdy and James Ruppert (Upper Saddle River, N.J.: Prentice Hall, 2000).

Library of Congress Cataloging-in-Publication Data

Owens, Louis.
I hear the train: reflections, inventions, refractions / Louis Owens.
p. cm. — (American Indian literature and critical studies series; v. 40)
Includes bibliographical references and index.
ISBN 0-8061-3354-6 (alk. paper)
1. Owens, Louis. 2. Indians of North America—Social life and customs. 3. Novelists, American—20th century—Biography. 4. Indian authors—United States—Biography. 5. Critics—United States—Biography. I. Title. II. Series.

PS3565.W567 Z467 2001
813'.54—dc21

2001027137

I Hear the Train: Reflections, Inventions, Refractions is Volume 40 in the American Indian Literature and Critical Studies Series.

The paper in this book meets the guidelines for permanence and durability of the Committee on Production Guidelines for Book Longevity of the Council on Library Resources, Inc. ∞

1 2 3 4 5 6 7 8 9 10

To Polly, Elizabeth, and Alexandra, with love

PART TWO. INVENTIONS

PART THREE. REFRACTIONS

Contents

Illustrations

All photos are from the author's collection.

Preface

This is a collection of stories, mostly true. Some are stories that arise from memory, stories of working on farms and ranches as a child and adolescent transplanted from Mississippi to California; of fighting fires or ranging a wilderness; or of a long journey to find my brother Gene after almost three decades of shrapnel-like silence and not-knowing; or of things that simply happened. Some are stories I've told myself in an attempt to fill in the empty places in memory and received history. Some are just stories, inventions, the kinds of fictions we create to make sense of the otherwise uninhabitable world we must, of necessity, inhabit; included in this category is a story called "Soul-Catcher," out of which my second novel grew long ago. Some are stories about others' stories, the sort of speculations we like to call criticism but know, truly, are just wistful readings of those stories given to us by the Creator's grace and our fellows' labor, the kinds of fictions a Nabokovian annotator might contrive in order to find his own beloved image in an otherwise alien text, with footnotes. Some are stories of pique and nostalgia for the unnamed realm glimpsed with our first emergence open eyed into our mother's world. Of course I must apologize for the kind of egocentrism reflected here, but as both Henry David Thoreau and Virginia Woolf said in different circumstances, if I knew anything else as well as I know myself, I would talk of that other.

In a box of photographs found after my older sister's young death, a box she had inherited from our mother at her own too-early death, are pictures taken of my mother's mixedblood Irish-Cherokee family in Oklahoma and, before that, Indian Territory. In a much-faded photo, my great-great uncle, August Edward Bailey, sits on railroad tracks in 1911 Oklahoma, a Cherokee-Irish mixed-blood between the rails en route to a hazy vanishing point in which ghosts of trees graze the blurred horizon, the narrowing rails the only definite demarcations. His railman's cap, with uneven brim, is cocked. His right arm rests nonchalantly upon his right knee. His face is dark and creased against the sun, the angular eyes typical of both my maternal and paternal families shut almost tight and pronounced lines descending from just below each eye to cheek bottom. He is very young, and his expression appears interested, a touch fatalistic, and perhaps a touch defiant as it is directed toward the camera. He wears a heavy glove on his right hand and holds the glove for his bare left hand in the right. Body language suggests a certain amount of satisfaction with his position in life and an equal awareness that others might not recognize his reasons for such satisfaction. Scrawled at the top of the photo is his name, "Augaust," misspelled. On the back of the photo-turned-postcard, in tall, slanting handwriting addressed to his mother, is this message: "this hant no count i will have a nothern one took and i will send you one so by by Augaust E."

I know next to nothing about Uncle August Edward Bailey, my mother's grandfather's brother. He was born poor in a rough country, worked for the railroad, had little formal education, was half-Indian in Indian Territory and the brand new state of Oklahoma, and has been dead for a very long time. My grandmother, orphaned at age six through means neither she nor we ever understood, could not tell us about this uncle. My mother, product of the worst margins of Uncle August's world and tumbled into a motherless world herself as a child, imbibed no stories that would answer such questions. Irish-American with Cherokee blood, American Indian with Irish blood, transient, infinitely motion-bent, poised within the tracks of an America determined to hurl all lives and stories toward a receding horizon, Uncle August and all the rest are particles scattered, the chaos of invasion, coloniality, deracination, and removal embedded in their blood and photographs. Like Uncle August, we are all between the tracks, framed by a vanishing point but satisfied and defiant to the end.

In another photo Uncle August stands in front of a small, mud-chinked log house with his mother, brothers, and sisters, a teenager sullenly confronting the camera. In another, on the back of a postcard photo of main-street Muldrow, Oklahoma, in 1913, also addressed to his mother, he writes, "I her the train so Bee good tell I see you." I, too, hear the train. Unseen, it rushes along shining tracks bracketing Uncle August in memory that arrives out of the dark and disappears at the vanishing point of convergence in a photograph. My inheritance, it leaves in the air a trace out of which I will construct history, mirroring consciousness, an irresolute "nothern one" that has been "took" and incessantly retaken. Though it may indeed be true that it "hant no good," it is nonetheless the invaluable stuff of story. Like that dollop of sourdough left behind in the bowl to double infinitely into another loaf, it becomes stories that birth others. And, as Vladimir Nabokov knew and showed us so brilliantly in his novel *Pale Fire*, we make stories in order to find ourselves at home in a chaos made familiar and comforting through the stories we make, searching frantically for patterns in the flux of randomly recorded events, a world in which endings stalk us and we can only keep inventing ways to both explain and forestall closure. Language must be the surest way, as we remain here telling ourselves stories in the dark, spinning webs of language against ever-encroaching myriad history like Faulkner, or writing ourselves into pages that read themselves out in the endings of our various selves like García Márquez, or laying a terrifying balm of language over the abyss of history like Cormac McCarthy— or writing back toward the center like N. Scott Momaday, Leslie Silko, James Welch, Gerald Vizenor, Thomas King, Louise Erdrich, and so many others.

Another photograph in my sister's box shows a strange, shanty-like "houseboat" my mother's mother lived on when she was very young, perhaps six or eight years old. I've written about that photograph elsewhere, but I cannot escape it. What story can that picture tell me and my eight brothers and sisters about the labyrinth of memory that should and must be our own? How may we, Kinbote-like, fill in the empty pages of the oral tradition that is all we have from our mother's world? Conscious of my own temerity in such an endeavor, I wrote that story and include it here: "Blessed Sunshine," the name of the shanty-boat. Similarly, I have gone back, in a fiction I call "Yazoo Dusk," to reconstruct, or construct for the first time, a story of the Mississippi my father's Choctaw-Irish-French family knew.

Because I cannot do less, I have made these various stories, call them essay, fiction, or criticism. Together, I believe they form a pattern, one turn and twist of the labyrinth leading to another. At the center, of course, is the hybrid monster of self, the ultimate cannibal to which all stories lead.

Acknowledgments

It is impossible to acknowledge all who have provided friendship, encouragement, and invaluable advice, but it is a pleasure to be able to thank at least a few: Gerald Vizenor, Kim Wiar, Karen Wieder, Irene Vernon, David Mogen, Jacquelyn Kilpatrick, Aaron Carr, Tom King, Evelina Lucero, Tom Colonnese, Elvira Pulitano, Luci Tapahonso, Gretchen Ronnow, Dan Obrien, Marci Rosenthal, Gretchen Bataille, Jesse Peters, Hossein Ordoubadian, Gail Jardine, Lauret Savoy, John Purdy, Jim Houston, Jack Hicks, Geary Hobson, Bernie Smith, the famous Mississippean James McElroy, and finally, of course, the Prescott Hotshots and Milk Creek Trail Crew.

PART ONE

Reflections

CHAPTER ONE

Finding Gene

A Black man, a figure of angles and pressed creases, bends to pull a weed, his white hair sharp against the dark, mown grass. Still bent, he looks up from the grave as my brother and I drive past below. The cemetery is on a hillside, worn stones and new-painted wooden crosses appearing to tilt beneath the thin oak and pine forest and the old man on the verge of tumbling head-over-heels down to our road. The waist-high picket fence that surrounds the little graveyard doesn't look sturdy enough to catch a falling body. I've never seen this hill country before, the woods everywhere outside the fence so thick and dark that they hold permanent shadow. I've never driven this narrow, broken road or breathed the moist Ozark air. Until today, I haven't seen my brother for twenty-nine years.

"That's the colored graveyard," Gene says. The three-quarter-ton pickup rattles and sends gravel pinging from mud tires. A red deer, of a color I've never seen in deer, freezes in a pasture on the other side of the road, studies us intently, and then with two strides vanishes into a brushy creek bottom. Deer hunting was something we used to have in common. We'd awaken in the dark and drive out to the low grain-covered Gabilan Mountains east of the Salinas Valley to be ready when the sun rose. Decades later I still smell the sweet, damp odor of oats and oak leaves and see the soft hawk ridges coming into focus at dawn. By midday those hills would be hot and burning with light, the clusters and lines of oaks black on ridges and in dry arroyos. I haven't hunted in nearly three decades, since I left the Gabilan and Santa Lucia mountains for college, but now I wonder if he hunts these red deer and I store the question for later use.

"You mean they're segregated?" I glance back and see the old man bent away from us now.

He shakes his head. "Nah. Just that they have their place and we have ours."

We, I think. In Mississippi and even at first in California, our only or best friends had often been Black or, more rarely, Indian. My first memories are of Gene and junglelike woods that grew thick between our cabin and the deep-edged brown water of the Yazoo River. Three, four, five, and six years old, I followed him everywhere, swinging on muskadine vines and eating the acid-sweet purple fruit, climbing pecan trees that we called pee-cans, fishing in the endless, muddy current of the river, jumping in the wire-sided cotton trucks filled with white bolls. The washtub where I had to bathe in gray water after him, leaning toward the wood cookstove on cold Mississippi mornings. The log shed we'd check each morning to see what skins our father had nailed up during the night. The watermelons we stole with a gang of Black kids from a cluster of shacks deep in the woods, our grandfather's melons, swinging over a ravine and dropping half of the melons with pink explosions as we swung. But the watermelons were later, in Texas.

Over the years, though I had written about some of these things, I'd begun to wonder what had actually happened and what my imagination had simply formed into history and truth. Without Gene I had no touchstone to truth, no way of verifying memories. I know that we invent what we need to be true, imagining and rewriting until there is some kind of text that gives us back a self.

◆ ◆ ◆

I was surprised at how comfortable it felt to be riding beside him in the Ford pickup. After a couple of hours together following twenty-nine years apart, my brother and I were headed out once again to shoot guns. Guns were something we'd always had in common, something we both still liked to see, touch, talk about. A difference was that for most of the intervening years, I had owned or touched no guns, our mother having sold my rifles and shotguns while I was away at college. Another difference was that I had not used a gun to kill a human being.

The first thing I noticed that morning was his smile. I'd forgotten that Gene was the only one in the family who always smiled. We're a serious lot all in all, the nine of us kids, given, I'm afraid, to looking for the darker possibilities in life and usually finding them. If any one of us children had a reason not to smile, however, it was Gene. In childhood he had a couple of extra upper teeth, like fangs, that had grown in over his canines, so that his constant smile was peculiarly friendly and ferocious at the same time. I remember thinking as an adolescent that he fought his smile, tried to hide those strange extra teeth, but the smile overcame everything. The navy had fixed his teeth, and at first I'd been perplexed by the difference when he walked out of his house toward my small Toyota pickup that morning. At fifty-one he was still thick and powerful looking through the shoulders and chest, but a noticeable belly pushed at his loose flannel shirt. His light brown hair had receded to the sides and back, leaving his head bald and shining, an inheritance from our mother, whose Irish father had been bald as a hen's egg, and a premonition to me.

Gene had been my hero, the toughest and bravest person I'd ever known, and patient and gentle at the same time. The only person to ever run our high-school cross-country track barefoot, he'd forced his short-legged, stocky body to run those long miles, keeping pace with his lanky Osage friend who was the best runner in the county. Gene was almost a quarter Cherokee but didn't show a trace of Indian. Still, people who knew our family sometimes attributed his barefoot running to the fact he was "Indian." The reality was, of course, that he simply couldn't afford cross-country shoes. The money we made from summer and after-school jobs went for clothes and food, not frivolous things like running shoes.

"Yeah, I still don't like shoes," he said when he noticed me looking at his bare feet as I got out of my truck.

◆ ◆ ◆

My brother had meant to say goodbye. In the summer of '68 he'd come back from his third tour of duty in Vietnam and had stopped by the cabin I shared with a friend in Morro Bay, California. There was a noise one night, and my friend looked up to see Gene climbing through a window. Windows were safer than doors, and surprise was safest of all. I was working evenings and wasn't there, so I didn't see him. He left that same night, telling no one where he was going, but I held close to the fact that he'd come to say goodbye at least, for we had grown up together, best friends who learned to hunt together, from slingshots to shotguns and deer rifles and recurve bows, to fish together, to set snares and traps in the hills and dry Salinas River bottom in California, to rebuild engines in the front yard and deal with a complicated family life that had taken us from Mississippi to California and back, and back again. Out of nine children, he was the second oldest, two years younger than our oldest sister and two years older than me. I was grown and living alone before I consciously realized that my older brother and sister had had a different father than the rest of us. In large families children often tend to break off into pairs or groupings. Gene and I grew up side by side, and then he graduated from high school and went to Vietnam, part of the first detachment of Swift Boat crewmen sent over after being told they had a probable survival rate of 10 percent.

◆ ◆ ◆

I'd arrived just before noon, driving down from Missouri, where I'd left my wife and two daughters with my wife's relatives at their family vacation house. It had taken half a day to penetrate that tangled Ozark country, through Branson with its traffic jam of billboards announcing over-the-hill country artists, a Liberace-like Asian violinist and his voluptuous blonde vocalists, and the Cherokee mixedblood, Wayne Newton. Over Lookout Mountain, a name vaguely resonant of the Civil War, and down into this remote part of western Arkansas.

♦ ♦ ♦

We'd exchanged only a few words, the tenuous language of careful greeting, when he began to show me his guns. I was a university professor who wrote books, and my brother molded inner tubes in a Firestone factory forty miles away from his little town. He'd been the first in the entire history of our families on both parents' sides to graduate from high school; I had been the second and last, and I was still the only one to ever enter college. In different ways Gene and I had vanished into new worlds a long way from home at almost the same time. I had kept in touch with family, calling and occasionally visiting, feeling sometimes like a time traveler beamed into an awkward past, while Gene had simply disappeared.

♦ ♦ ♦

He unlocked a big closet and began to bring out guns. A pair of 12-gauge pumps; a long-barreled, bolt-action 12-gauge "goose-gun" that had belonged to our father; a .410 and two 20-gauges; an ancient 10-gauge; two identical lever-action .30-30s; a couple of .30-ought-6s; a .30-40 Krag like one our father still hunted with in California; a beautiful Browning 20-gauge over-and-under for quail; three black-powder rifles; a .22 magnum; a .222, a .243, a .270. Then he began to bring out the handguns: 9 millimeters, .40 calibers, a pair of .357s, a .44 magnum, .22-caliber target pistols. He laid out his compound bow, an ugly contrivance that had little to do with the beautiful Bear recurves we'd hunted with as teenagers. I remembered the last time I'd hunted with a bow, when I'd pinned a rabbit to a tree and watched the little thing spin screaming around the arrow shaft. It takes great pain to cause a rabbit or deer to scream, and either is a sound you don't forget. He hunted deer every fall, he said when I asked, stalking one particularly fine buck the last few seasons. For several years in a row he had tracked the large-antlered buck, set his scope on it, and never fired. The time and place or the feeling in the air were never quite right, he explained. Maybe next year, or the one after that, it would feel right. In all of his years in the Ozarks—all the years since Vietnam—I finally realized, he had never actually killed a deer. It was the hunting that counted, the knowledge that he could think and feel like them, ease into their world, *be* the deer for a privileged time once each year just before winter set in. I remembered the feeling from that old life we'd shared.

◆ ◆ ◆

I hefted and aimed down barrels at peep sights and into darkened scopes, lifted and lined up pistols, spoke softly in terms of admiration and awe, conscious even at the time that guns had become, on this strange day in Arkansas, the *petites madeleines* of our own remembrance of things past, and even thinking of it with that absurd, stuffed-shirt Proustian term.

◆ ◆ ◆

With a dozen handguns we climbed into his pickup, heading for the target range a few minutes from his house, passing the cemetery with its old caretaker, and finding upon arrival that we had the range all to ourselves. We hung targets and I went first, hitting a dead-center bullseye at twenty yards on my first shot with the .44 magnum. Immediately, I put the gun down.

Gene grinned at me. Neither of us said the obvious, that my bullseye with the .44 was a wild moment straight out of chaos theory, that I couldn't do it again in twenty years. As kids we'd had shooting competitions that I'd usually won. But he'd spent three years in Vietnam, patrolling the Mekong Delta and the coast on a Swift Boat, sometimes leaving the water to go on foot into jungle that I could only imagine as a vague and evil dream. Later he explained that he'd shot a child, a little girl running toward them with a satchel charge while his CO shouted at him to fire. That was when all the pieces began to separate for him. Nothing fit any longer. I had refused induction because of him, because of his letters home, had been drafted and ultimately kept from prison at the last minute by Richard Nixon. With the war winding down Nixon had canceled the draft for my quarter, sparing all of us who had been or were about to be inducted or imprisoned. My brother had still been in Vietnam at the time. To this day, though I know I did the morally right thing, a tiny, mean abscess of guilt works at me. I should have gone where my brother was.

For three hours we shot handguns, changing targets and picking up empty casings. The next day, he promised, we were going catfishing.

His house was small and dark, on the edge of that lost Ozark town of fifteen hundred people. He kept the shades drawn, the windows and doors locked, a .38 pistol in a drawer beside his bed beneath a stack of four novels I had written. Proudly, he showed me the banana trees he grew in front of the house. Each fall he dug them up, wrapped roots in canvas, and put them under his house to survive the winter for spring replanting. Diminutive bananas grew in a bunch on each of the two trees. With undisguised pain he showed me the empty pen where he'd kept his bird dog, an English Setter, until it died that summer. When I told him that I was now on my third English Setter over a span of twenty-five years, he nodded without surprise, though neither of us had ever even heard of such dogs growing up.

The next morning we went fishing on neighbors' farms. For many years I had been a fly-fisherman, tying bits of feather and strands of hair into miniscule imitations that might trick rainbow trout in clear, fragile-looking waters. At the murky farm ponds, we put globs of rancid chicken liver on big hooks and cast with fifteen-pound test line and large sinkers just as we had many years before. Casting far out toward the pond's center, I felt a weight of old and familiar satisfaction as the thick monofilament sang off my open reel. The plunk at the end was solid and gratifying, and nothing, I knew, could ever break my over-heavy line. When a catfish bit, it was a sudden, determined pull—a direct communication— nothing like the wary rise and tentative strike of a rainbow trout.

At the first farm I caught and released a small blue cat on almost every cast, while Gene caught nothing. We moved to a second pond on someone else's property, where we both caught fat two- and three-pound yellow-brown mudcats one after another until we had a good mess of fish. At home he filleted them and his wife fried them in cornmeal.

I could tell she was happy to see me. A tough, wiry Arkansas woman who had probably saved my brother, coaxing him out of the deep woods into town and out of alcohol madness into a semblance of normal life. When she smoked, he made her sit in a small corral made up of four huge air purifiers in a sequestered corner of the living room. Like me, he hated smoking with an intensity my own wife calls neurotic. But his wife Carol laughed about it, just as she laughed when he brought out a box of Vietnam mementos to show me, including photographs of beautiful bar girls sitting on his lap. "I bought that one for a week," he said, pointing to a stunningly lovely and very young-looking girl. As I studied the photo, his wife shook her head in disgust, and there was an edge of wonder in his own voice, too, as if he were talking about someone else and something that had absolutely nothing to do with a real world where one might be responsible for one's own life. In a matter-of-fact way, his wife interrupted to explain that he'd nearly killed her a few months earlier when she moved during the night unexpectedly.

"Gene still has his problems," she said, looking at him with what struck me as critical love.

He shook his head, closing the box. "I used to have a bunch of medals and stuff," he said. "I wonder what happened to them."

When I told him I'd come across them recently in our mother's old trunk at the home of one of our younger sisters, he looked surprised.

"I guess I'd like to see those," he said, without much conviction.

I promised to call our sister, thinking of the medals I'd seen tangled in the tin trunk with the residue of our mother's short life. Just before disappearing, he'd discarded the medals and she'd collected them for the future. Now they were in the cheap, much dented trunk with sixty-year-old postcards from our reckless grandmother, a picture frame made out of Camel cigarette packages by our Uncle Bob in prison, ancient silk scarves sent home from the war in the Pacific, currency from the Japanese-occupied Philippines brought back somehow by a second uncle who'd been on Bataan. Both of those uncles, our mother's and father's only brothers, had been murdered years after coming home. Neither case had been solved, or perhaps even investigated. I wondered if Gene knew something about our uncles, but I didn't ask.

Sitting there after catfish and fried potatoes, I was able, however, to ask the question that had clawed at me for years: Why had he re-upped twice? Why had he stayed three years in what his letters had described as worse than any hell a person could imagine? He looked at me directly when he answered, his brown eyes locking on mine for the first time since I'd come to his home. "I stayed so that someone wouldn't have to take my place," he said.

♦ ♦ ♦

I had thought he was dead. I suppose we all had, though perhaps our older sister had known his secret and kept it. I don't know. She has been diagnosed with terminal cancer at age fifty-three, with very little time left, and our conversations are cautious and precise. We sit and talk of childhood, inventing memories and humorous recollections, but I don't ask her about secrets. Gene had left for the same war I had planned to go to before his warnings, and then he'd come back only to vanish. It was as though he'd never come back at all, as though they'd killed him and sent something else home.

♦ ♦ ♦

That's how I'd come to be in Arkansas, just a few miles from the Oklahoma town where our Cherokee grandmother was born. I'd written a novel about my brother. My second novel, *The Sharpest Sight*, was born out of Gene's disappearance, out of the paradox of his nonreturn from that war. "The arrows of death fly unseen at noon-day; the sharpest sight can't discern them," the book's epigraph read. It was a book about Mississippi, about my father's Choctaw ancestors, about the mysteries of identity and story, but most of all it was a book about a lost brother and a long pattern of loss into which that one seemed to fit. I'd made a journey to the black wall in Washington, D.C., and found the names of friends who'd died in Vietnam, but I'd had no idea where my own brother's name might be found, so I'd made a story out of what I did not know.

And then one day, after a quarter of a century of silence, my brother called. He had found a copy of *The Sharpest Sight*, had seen my name and read the book. This was extraordinary, because Gene does not go into bookstores and does not usually read books. But he had read it and had known at once that it was about him, had read past layers of metaphor and myth, through a complex "mystery" plot, to see that I'd written a novel about the loss of my own brother.

He located and called our older sister and got my phone number from her. "Jesus Christ," he'd said to her, "first he put me in a mental hospital and then he killed me. What's he going to do to me next?" Or words to that effect. Then he called me.

It took three years to convince him to let me visit. Usually when I'd phone he wouldn't be home. He did not answer letters. He almost came to our mother's funeral, he said, but in the end he couldn't. We'd talk maybe twice a year and I'd say that I might be in the area and would like to drop by. He'd like that, he'd say, but time was short, he was working double shifts at the tire plant, there were problems with his wife's two grown children whom he'd adopted. Finally, he'd said I should come.

"You remember the time that panther got on the roof?" he asked as we were sitting in his living room.

My mind jumped at the memory, for that long-ago event had made a nightmare that stalked me through childhood into adulthood and become an image and theme that haunted my writing. I had thought, dreamed, and written about it so much, and so indirectly, that I'd come to wonder if I'd invented it. Had a black cougar, a "painter," followed our father out of the swamps one night to leap upon the roof of our little cabin and scream its rage? Had we children cowered in the two-room cabin listening to the cat's feet on tin roof and screams like an angry and terrified woman's? Was the black cat that became *nalusachito,* the soul-eater in my writing and the black thing that turned dream into terror, a real memory?

"You remember that?" I asked.

"Course. I remember it jumped down and whipped our dog. What was that dog's name? That coon hound."

I shook my head, unable to recall the cat's fight with an either very brave or very foolish dog and not even remembering that particular dog because there had been too many back then.

"Did it kill our dog?" I asked.

He shook his head. "Didn't even hurt him too bad as I recall."

So the cat must have wanted to leave. But why had it stalked our father to the cabin and leapt onto the roof, knocking the tin chimney off in its rage? I knew that Choctaws had stories of such panthers. They were female and they were more than animal. They sought a person out for a dark purpose and were more than feared. Maybe that had been the beginning of the change that had sent our father into whatever kind of strange reality he inhabited these many years later, maybe the reason he stared out at the world with the eyes of a curious but disinterested child and merely looked with vague curiosity when he met his grandchildren for the first time. More likely, the truck accident and two-week coma he'd been in when I was fifteen had changed him, not *nalusachito.* But one never knows.

"Do you remember stealing watermelons with those Black kids and swinging over that ravine with them?"

He grinned. "I always thought we were getting away with it, but I found out Grampa was just letting us do it." He looked into himself for a moment and grinned again. "You remember when we used to go hunting and not come home till the next day? Just cook a rabbit over a fire and sleep out?"

I remembered. I remembered for the first time since the moment itself the day we'd found a squash growing wild in the river bottom and Gene had cut up and eaten the whole thing on the spot, raw. He could eat or drink anything, crouching to lap water from a stream or trough when thirsty. I don't remember him ever having a stomachache, while all the time I was in a constant state of pain, my stomach knotted around barbed wire for the first forty years of my life.

I felt almost dizzy with the reality of memory. Old memories had become both more real and changed in the same moment. Did he remember me almost drowning us when I shoved the old shattered rowboat into the Yazoo current with several of us kids in it? Did he remember the time a bear chased Rex, our Border collie, onto the porch? Did he remember stealing hundred-pound sacks of almonds in California? The time our father's deer rifle went off and the bullet went through our mother's hair into the kitchen ceiling? Did he recall all of the things I would not put into words?

That night we sat up late, remembering. In the morning I couldn't recall dreaming, and I lay in bed for a time wondering what he really thought of the stories I'd written, using the raw material of our lives for fantastic fictions. I wrote about Indian things, and Gene didn't identify as Indian. His father had been German, not Choctaw, and our mother's Cherokee world was remote from him. He liked my fiction, clearly, was proud that I'd written it and he was part of it, but how had he felt seeing himself imagined that way?

On the third day we shook hands awkwardly and I got into my pickup to drive back to New Mexico. "Just a second," he said with a jerk of his head. He went back into the house and came out holding one of the lever-action .30-30s in his right hand.

"You better take this with you. That way we'll both have one." He smiled. "This too, since you're the fisherman in the family." In his other hand he held a wooden bass lure our father had carved in his own youth. Only bare traces of paint remained on the clumsy-looking plug with which our father had caught many fish.

One day, I thought as I drove away, I'd like my daughters to meet their uncle. Maybe then they'd know their father better. Perhaps their memories would become more real.

Crossing into Oklahoma, I stopped in Muldrow, where our grandmother had been born, and then went up to Tahlequah, a place she and our mother had often spoken of. My wife and children would return from Missouri in a couple of days, but for now I was alone, driving through Indian country and thinking of Gene, planning to send him the beaded rifle scabbard a Creek friend had made for me, for Gene was the hunter in the family. "Indian Country," my brother had said, was what they'd called enemy territory during the war. Out there, in Indian country, anything could happen. A person might never get home.

CHAPTER TWO

Bracero Summer

The summer of '65 was shaping up to be something. Things had been happening all year. The Salinas River had flooded especially high that winter at our end of the Salinas Valley, tearing out garages and barns and anything it could reach and rafting everything up to Monterey. When the river went down, my brother shot a fifteen-pound steelhead with his .22 right behind our house and then, with a few friends, went off to a war called Vietnam, leaving me his green metal-flake '57 Chevy with a 283 bored out to 301, twin Holly four-barrel carbs, three-quarter cam, Herst four-on-the-floor, button-and-tuck upholstery, four-eleven rear end, and mag rims. The Beatles and Beach Boys were so popular that buddies of mine wore Nehru jackets and Beatles haircuts or flashed madras shirts and huaraches and drove "woodies" with surfboards sticking out the back. Some guys on the wrestling team in our little school of three hundred small-town kids had pushed the basketball coach's car, a 40-something Dodge, off a fifty-foot cliff into the creek that ran through the school. The coach was a Choctaw Indian and very popular with students. Destroying his car was widely recognized as an act of affection. A guy I played basketball with had worked hard all of one night to paint out a billboard on the highway that ran through the middle of town, replacing the ad with a plea for all of us to vote for him as God. Another acquaintance had stolen an airplane from the next town over and dropped empty bottles from his case of beer on our town's only hamburger stand, and a guy one year behind me in school had dug up his grandmother from the cemetery on the hill to drive around town with her corpse draped across the hood of his pickup. Tommy Outhouse—his real name—had borrowed and rolled Hobie Joe's Volkswagen van over on the highway to Morro Bay and then got out and lifted it single-handedly back onto its wheels before running away forever. Members of the Atascadero High School Letterman's Club had hijacked a rooter's bus from Paso Robles and held the occupants at gunpoint, threatening to execute all of them over a tough football loss. One of my friends had inscribed his name in the town's history books by pole-vaulting his car over a pickup truck on a country road. He'd been steering the engineless car at an impressive speed when the front end of the wired-up driveshaft had dropped right into a cattle guard. The drive shaft stuck and the car lifted and soared onto the back of the pickup towing it. I was seventeen years old and in good shape from basketball, running in the sandy river bottom every night, part-time work at the mushroom farm, and odd jobs on various ranches around the county. Even before school was out, the sun was bright and hot and the Pacific Ocean just twenty miles away. But I wasn't thinking of the ocean; I was reflecting on the harsh probabilities of another summer shoveling mushroom compost or bucking hay or building fence to buy gas for a car that rocked and growled when it idled and got seven miles per gallon.

The southern end of the Salinas Valley was a pressure cooker. People too young to go to Vietnam yet were looking for something to do in the meantime, and most of the time that something was each other. Girls' mascara ran in the sweaty heat and miniskirts stuck to damp thighs. Boys cruised town with our shirts off, arms out '57 Chevy windows and Wolfman Jack on the radio playing loud from KAFY over in Bakersfield. Gary Morales, one of the most gentle souls in town, fell out of the back of a truck and got a two-inch scar on his cheek and became mean, picking fights nearly every day and winning. Out on the chicken and turkey farms the birds were panting in the stagnant air, and on the oat-hill ranches all the whiteface cattle were bunched beneath live oaks for shade.

Black people had rioted in American cities the summer before, going absolutely ballistic over things I knew little about. They'd burned buildings and looted and scared the hell out of white people and politicians. With another hot summer coming up, important people in Sacramento, the state capital, were worried, and rightfully so as it turned out, for 1965 was to be the summer of the notorious Watts Riots. Meanwhile, in 1964 the federal government had abruptly ended the "Bracero" program that for two decades had brought millions of workers from Mexico to harvest U.S. crops, mostly in California. Almost two hundred thousand Braceros had entered the U.S. in 1963, down from the nearly half-million who had been coming each year during the last half of the '50s and early '60s, but still a lot by some people's count. There was genuine fear that our high standard of culture and civic values might be undermined by so many Mexicans coming in. By 1965, with the program ended, the number of Mexican workers entering was down to twenty thousand, and two years later only seven thousand came. Illegals took care of most of the labor shortage, and at a real savings to corporate farmers, but despite illegals some growers were feeling the pinch.

While in our little town of Atascadero at the southern end of the Salinas Valley we were busy stealing planes, digging up our grandmothers, destroying the coach's car, and pointing magnum pistols at occupants of rooters' buses, men in Sacramento were thinking. Two birds with one stone, they thought. Summer was about to open like one of those anticipated blockbusters in a city near everyone. Vietnam was coming to a rapid boil and draft-age boys and their sisters and girlfriends were starting to wake up on college campuses if not yet in Atascadero. Black people with little to lose in California's cities—just like the rest of the country—were mad and ready to cause some serious problems for people who had a lot to lose. At the same time there was a minor shortage of Mexican